Nina the Neighborhood Ninja

Sonia Panigrahy

Illustrated by Hazel Quintanilla

Nina the Neighborhood Ninja

For information about this title or to order other books and/or electronic media, contact the publisher:

Tiny Sparks Press
http://www.soniapanigrahy.com
tinysparkspress@gmail.com

Library of Congress Control Number: 2016917385

ISBNs:

English hardcover: 978-0-9975956-1-1
English eBook: 978-0-9975956-6-6
English softcover: 978-0-9975956-0-4

Spanish hardcover: 978-0-9975956-2-8
Spanish eBook: 978-0-9975956-3-5
Spanish softcover: 978-0-9975956-4-2

Printed in the United States of America

Cover and interior design: 1106 Design, LLC
Illustrated by Hazel Michelle Quintanilla Campos

This book belongs to:

_____

This book is dedicated
to my niece,
Jahnavi,
and my two nephews,
Alekh and Rohan.

Nina is the Neighborhood Ninja.

She is smart.

She is strong.

She is speedy.

No one can get in Nina the Ninja's way

when a rescue is needed.

Well, except for her sidekick, Fiona the Firefly.

Fiona does not really get in the way, but she knows

how to help. Just at the right time.

Just in the right way.

Most days are pretty calm in the neighborhood.

But today was a totally different story.

Totally different.

I mean, Nina the Ninja had never seen

anything like it before.

You know—it's like those days when everything

seems to happen all at once.

The morning started when Nina the Ninja
was playing soccer with some kids in a park.
She heard a distressed peeping sound
in the tree above her. She decided to investigate.
She saw a baby bird on the ground
at the bottom of the tree.

Nina the Ninja needed to think fast!

How could she help the baby bird?

She figured it out!

Nina the Ninja folded her cape,

made knots on both ends of it

to create a sling.

She gently placed the baby bird inside.

She climbed the tree

to safely return the baby bird

to its happy mother.

The neighborhood is lucky

that Nina is smart

and strong

and speedy.

Nina the Ninja

and Fiona the Firefly

celebrated their success

of rescuing the baby bird and

returning it to its mother.

Thinking so quickly

and climbing trees

takes a lot of energy!

They celebrated by having

the most incredible picnic.

Nina the Ninja
noticed that the sky
was getting dark and that
stormy clouds were
rolling in overhead.
She needed to get home fast,
before the rain
started to come down.

While they were running home
to beat the storm,
Nina the Ninja saw a cat,
looking scared.
The cat did not have any shelter.
Nina the Ninja knew that cats
don't like to get wet and
that the cat needed a shelter.
First, she needed to find
some materials.

Nina the Ninja
knew she needed
to build a shelter
that would stand strong
against the rain
and the wind,
but she had to do it quickly—
before the storm got worse!

As the raindrops started falling

from the sky to the ground,

Nina the Ninja

and Fiona the Firefly

finished the shelter—just in time.

Another success!

The neighborhood is lucky

that Nina is smart

and strong

and speedy.

Nina the Ninja

and Fiona the Firefly

needed to get home!

They waved back at the cat

that was now safe and warm

in the new house.

The rain started to come down heavily.

They were almost home.

Wait a second . . .

she noticed something strange

in the sandbox

in the playground.

A family of turtles
was stuck in the sand!
Nina the Ninja was tired and cold
and wet and hungry.
She had to decide between running home
to be warm and dry
or saving the family of turtles
from sinking in the sand.
But, it was clear
what had to be done.
The turtles had to be saved!

Fiona the Firefly held

Nina the Ninja's cape

over her head to protect Nina

and the turtles against the rain.

Nina the Ninja pulled each turtle out,

one by one.

The turtles were out of the sandbox

and safe from danger!

Luckily, they have their own shelters —

their shells! — for protection

against the storm.

The neighborhood is lucky

that Nina is smart

and strong

and speedy.

Nina the Ninja

and Fiona the Firefly

had a long and busy day.

But, they knew it was

a great day, too!

Many animals were now able to be safe

because Nina the Ninja was smart,

courageous, brave, and strong.

Let's not forget Fiona the Firefly!

Fiona knew how to help.

Just at the right time.

Just in the right way.

When they reached home,
they took a warm bath.

Nina the Ninja and Fiona the Firefly ate their dinner,

and, finally, the rain started to slow down.

Nina the Ninja

and Fiona the Firefly

were exhausted after

a long day of rescue missions,

but they were relieved that

they were able to help so many

of their new friends.

Their new friends

wanted to show appreciation

by coming to Nina the Ninja's house

to do something nice for them.

They decide to celebrate
a successful day together.

Afterward, it was time to get some rest, because who knew what tomorrow might bring?

How are **YOU** going to use
your superpowers tomorrow?
Do you have superpowers?

Are you smart?
(Yes!)

Are you strong?
(Yes!)

Are you speedy?
(Yes!)

The world is lucky
to have another superhero
to help save the day.